Make friends with

Sheltie

The little pony with the big heart

Sheltie is the lovable little Shetland pony with a big personality. His best friend and owner is Emma, and together they have lots of exciting adventures.

Share Sheltie and Emma's adventures in

SHELTIE THE SHETLAND PONY
SHELTIE SAVES THE DAY
SHELTIE AND THE RUNAWAY
SHELTIE FINDS A FRIEND
SHELTIE TO THE RESCUE
SHELTIE IN DANGER
SHELTIE RIDES TO WIN
SHELTIE AND THE SADDLE MYSTERY
SHELTIE LEADS THE WAY
SHELTIE THE HERO
SHELTIE IN TROUBLE
SHELTIE AND THE STRAY
SHELTIE AND THE SNOW PONY
SHELTIE ON PARADE

Peter Clover was born and went to school in London. He was a storyboard artist and illustrator before he began to put words to his pictures. He enjoys painting, travelling, cooking and keeping fit, and lives on the coast in Somerset.

Also by Peter Clover in Puffin

The Sheltie series

Sheltie
For Ever

Peter Clover

PUFFIN BOOKS

For Vanessa and Ian Davie

PUFFIN BOOKS

Published by the Penguin Group
Penguin Books Ltd, 27 Wrights Lane, London W8 5TZ, England
Penguin Putnam Inc., 375 Hudson Street, New York, New York 10014, USA
Penguin Books Australia Ltd, Ringwood, Victoria, Australia
Penguin Books Canada Ltd, 10 Alcorn Avenue, Toronto, Ontario, Canada M4V 3B2
Penguin Books (NZ) Ltd, Private Bag 102902, NSMC, Auckland, New Zealand

Penguin Books Ltd, Registered Offices: Harmondsworth, Middlesex, England

First published 1999
1 3 5 7 9 10 8 6 4 2

Copyright © Working Partners Ltd, 1999
All rights reserved

Created by Working Partners Ltd, London, W12 7QY

The moral right of the author has been asserted

Set in 14/22 Palatino

Made and printed in England by Clays Ltd, St Ives plc

British Library Cataloguing in Publication Data
A CIP catalogue record for this book is available from the British Library

ISBN 0–141–30450–2

Chapter One

'Where's Emma got to?' said Mum, leaning out of the kitchen window. 'I told her to post those letters then come straight back for her tea!'

Dad was home and playing in the garden with little Joshua.

'I expect she'll be back shortly,' Dad said. He leaned over the gate and looked up the lane. 'Yes, here she comes now. And it looks as though she's riding a rocket.'

Emma and Sheltie, her little Shetland pony, came thundering down the lane at a lightning gallop. They skidded to a halt with a clatter of hoofs, just outside the back gate.

'Whoever it is you're racing, Emma, you've left them miles behind,' laughed Dad. Joshua bounded over to the fence to see Sheltie. The little pony was puffing and blowing after his race back from the village.

Emma's face looked hot and red as she leaped from the saddle and took up Sheltie's reins.

'It's Barrow Hill,' cried Emma breathlessly. 'They're going to knock the top off and flatten it to build the new road.'

'What?' said Dad.

'There's a notice up outside the post

2

office and everyone's talking about it,' continued Emma. 'They can't flatten Barrow Hill, can they, Dad?' Emma sounded very worried.

'I wouldn't have thought so,' said Dad. 'Barrow Hill is part of Little Applewood. And anyway, the new road is planned to go *around* the hill, not *over* it.'

Mum came outside to see what all the fuss was about.

'That can't be right, Emma,' Mum said when she'd heard Emma's story. 'It's such a pretty hill and everyone looks out on to it from their windows.'

It was true. Barrow Hill sat nicely in the background, nestling between Beacon Hill and the woods behind Mr Brown's meadow. Little Applewood just wouldn't be the same without it.

'But there's a notice and everything,' continued Emma. 'Half the village is outside the post office signing a petition. What's a petition, Dad?'

'It's a list which people put their names to if they don't agree with something,' explained Dad.

'Well, I think we should all go down there straight away and add our names,' said Emma.

'Definitely,' said Mum. 'We'll go down to the village as soon as we've had our tea.'

After tea they all went to the village as planned. And Emma was right. A big notice was pasted in the post office window, outlining the council's change of plan to re-route the new road.

Sheltie pushed his way through a crowd

of people as Mum read the notice. 'It says that the old chalk pit cut into the back of the hill is crumbling away. And the council think it would be better if the hill was levelled off completely, and the new road taken directly over the top.'

'That's nonsense,' exclaimed one of the villagers. 'The chalk pit isn't crumbling away at all.'

'Chalk's meant to be soft,' said another. 'And the pit has been there for years. The only reason they want to build the road over the hill instead of going the long way around it is because it will cost less.'

'They wouldn't dare do it if the chalk pony still grazed there,' said Mr Crock mysteriously. But nobody except Emma seemed to hear him.

'They shouldn't be allowed to get away with it,' said Mum. 'Come on. Let's sign this petition.'

Chapter Two

The next day was Saturday, and Emma had
arranged to meet up with Sally and her
pony, Minnow. Emma was anxious to tell
her best friend the terrible news about
Barrow Hill and the plans for the new road.

'It's awful news,' agreed Sally.

Sheltie blew a loud harrumph.

'I think Sheltie agrees too!' Sally
continued. The little pony pawed at the
ground then looked up at his friend,

7

Minnow. 'Riding over the hill won't be the same if there's a noisy road with lots of traffic,' she moaned. Sally stroked Minnow's neck and looked at Emma.

'Mr Crock said that they wouldn't dare do it if the chalk pony still grazed there,' said Emma.

'Chalk pony?' quizzed Sally. 'What chalk pony?'

'I don't know,' puzzled Emma. 'It was just something that Mr Crock said. But maybe we should go and see him and find out!'

Sheltie and Minnow trotted along side by side on their way to Mr Crock's cottage. Being smaller than Minnow, Sheltie had to move his little legs extra fast, just to keep up.

The two girls rode right up to Mr Crock's

garden gate. But when they looked out for Emma's neighbour, he was nowhere to be seen.

They left their two ponies tethered loosely to the gatepost and knocked at Mr Crock's door. When no one answered, Emma pushed the door and found that it was open.

'Hello! Mr Crock!' called Emma. 'Are you home?'

There was no answer, so Emma pushed the door further and peered inside into the hallway.

She could see the old wooden staircase and the cupboard below. The cupboard door was open and Mr Crock's legs were sticking out. His head was so far inside the cupboard that he couldn't hear Emma calling.

Emma and Sally stepped into the hallway. They could both hear Mr Crock mumbling and grumbling from inside the cupboard.

'I know it's in here somewhere!' he said. 'Probably right at the back.'

'Hello! Mr Crock. It's me, Emma. Is it all right to come in?'

'Who? Who's that?' Mr Crock crawled out of the cupboard backwards. 'Oh! It's you, Emma. And Sally.' He blinked in the bright sunshine that streamed through the door behind them.

Emma and Sally grinned and tried not to laugh out loud. Mr Crock was covered in fluff and cobwebs.

'We've come to ask you about the chalk pony,' said Emma. 'I was telling Sally about what you'd said outside the post

10

office. How the council wouldn't dare take the new road over the hill if the chalk pony was still there.'

Mr Crock pulled himself up on to his feet. He looked at Emma and Sally with a big grin.

'Well, that's a coincidence. I was just thinking about the chalk pony myself. I was almost certain there were some old photographs of it in an album, stored away somewhere in this cupboard. But I haven't found them yet.' He dragged a big cardboard box out into the hallway.

Outside, just at that moment, Sheltie gave a tremendous sneeze. His head jerked so suddenly that his reins came free of the gatepost. Sheltie didn't waste a second. He could hear Emma's voice coming from inside the cottage and trotted towards her immediately.

Chapter Three

Sheltie stood with his two front hoofs on the step and poked his head through the door into the hallway. The little pony huffed and puffed until they noticed he was there. Everyone was surprised by his sudden appearance.

'Sheltie!' exclaimed Emma. 'How did you get loose?' She grabbed the reins to stop him coming in any further and tried to head him away outside. But Sheltie was very interested in Mr Crock's cardboard box and seemed determined to take a closer look.

Emma pulled him away. And Sheltie pulled Emma back. Emma pulled again. And so did Sheltie.

'I think Sheltie wants a game of tug of war,' chuckled Mr Crock.

'More like nosy-in-the-box,' laughed Sally.

'Go on then, let him take a look, Emma,' smiled Mr Crock. He pushed the box towards Sheltie. 'He can't harm anything. And if he's looking for carrots he knows better than to think there might be any hidden in there.'

Emma slackened the reins and let Sheltie poke his head into the box of jumble. It was very dusty in there and

Sheltie gave another big sneeze.

'That'll teach you, nosy,' smiled Emma.

But Sheltie didn't mind a spot of dust.
He poked at a few things with his nose
then became interested in a large book
hidden underneath an old jumper. Sheltie
grabbed the book with his teeth and
dragged it out on to the floor.

Then Sheltie gave it a nudge with his
hoof and stood back proudly, showing off
his find.

'Well, would you believe it!' exclaimed
Mr Crock. 'That's just what I've been
looking for!'

Sheltie blew a soft whicker as Mr Crock
bent down and picked up the dusty photo
album.

'Clever Sheltie,' said Mr Crock.

He held up the album and blew a thick

layer of dust from its cover. This made Sheltie sneeze again.

'Bless you,' said Mr Crock. Then he opened the album and looked at the photographs inside. Emma and Sally stretched their necks for a better look.

There were lots of faded brown photos of Mr Crock in his younger days.

There were also some photos of Little Applewood and the surrounding countryside which were taken before Emma or her parents were even born.

'Is that you?' grinned Emma, pointing to a skinny boy in short trousers and hobnailed boots.

Mr Crock smiled. 'I've got legs like a knock-kneed sparrow, haven't I?'

Sally burst out laughing, and this set Sheltie off neighing loudly.

'It wasn't that funny,' said Mr Crock.

'It was,' grinned Emma.

There was one special photograph that made Emma and Sally gasp with surprise. It was a picture of the chalk pony grazing on Barrow Hill with three people standing in the foreground.

'There he his,' announced Mr Crock. 'The chalk pony up on the hill. That's what he used to look like all those years ago. And there's me with old Fred Berry and his cousin.'

Sheltie rested his head

on Emma's shoulder as she and Sally looked at the old photograph.

'How did the chalk pony get there?' asked Emma as she studied the white silhouette cut out of the hillside. It looked as though the chalk pony had been made with a giant pastry cutter, showing the clean white shape of a pony against the grassy hill.

'My grandfather told me it was cut hundreds of years ago, to bring luck to the village,' said Mr Crock. The chalk pony stood grazing and looked down from the hill over the rooftops of Little Applewood. 'Now, if Chalky was still there,' he continued, 'the council wouldn't dare bring the new road over the hill. It would have to go around, just like they had first planned.'

'But where's Chalky gone?' asked Emma. 'What happened to him?'

'He's disappeared over the years,' said Mr Crock sadly. 'Faded slowly with time so that no one has even noticed he's gone.'

'Maybe he's not gone!' said Emma brightly. 'Perhaps he's still there! What if he's just hiding beneath the grass and weeds, waiting to be found?'

She looked at Sally. Emma could tell that Sally was thinking the same thing.

'Come on, Sally. Let's go up there and see if we can find him. If anyone can save the hill, then Chalky can.'

Sheltie blew a tremendous snort as he nudged Emma outside, eager to get going.

Chapter Four

Once up on Barrow Hill, Emma and Sally began their search for the chalk pony. They rode to the spot in Mr Crock's photograph, where they thought Chalky might be, and slipped out of their saddles. Sheltie and Minnow were happy to graze freely while Emma and Sally combed the area on foot.

'It must be around here somewhere,' said Emma. She picked up a stick and began parting the weeds and thick brambles which grew there.

'I'll look over here,' said Sally. She found a stick too and began to search in a different spot.

The two girls scraped away at the grass but found nothing except brown earth. Then Sheltie became interested in what they were up to. He trotted over and joined in the search. First he watched Emma and Sally, then he copied what they were doing and pawed at the ground with his hoofs.

'Look at Sheltie,' said Sally. 'He's come to help.'

Sheltie was very keen, and quickly scraped away several holes in the grass. He made a terrible mess and sent grass and weeds flying everywhere.

Suddenly, a big clump of turf went sailing through the air and hit Emma's riding hat.

'Ow! Sheltie. Not so rough,' cried Emma. Then she noticed that the clump of turf was white underneath, and that Sheltie's hoofs were covered in chalk.

Sheltie tossed his head and let out a lively snort.

'Sally! I think Sheltie's found something,' called Emma.

Sally hurried over to see what Sheltie

had discovered. The little pony pawed at
the patch some more, and revealed a
hidden surface of white chalk beneath the
grass.

'This must be it!' exclaimed Sally
excitedly. 'Sheltie's found the chalk pony.'

Sheltie whinnied again and pranced on
the spot, pumping his little legs up and
down. Emma gave him a big hug. 'Well
done, boy. Well done!'

Minnow stood and watched as Emma,

Sally and Sheltie scraped away more grass and weeds. There was no stopping Sheltie now.

Eventually Sheltie uncovered a whole section which resembled the head of a pony.

'We've found it!' cried Emma. 'This is definitely Chalky. But we're going to need some help to clear away the rest, Sally. There's so much of it.'

'Why don't we go and tell Mr Crock?' suggested Sally. 'He'll know what to do.'

'And I'm sure Mum and Dad will help,' added Emma. 'They were really angry when they found out about the new plans for the road. I bet everyone in the village will want to help too!'

Emma and Sally rode as fast as they could back down to the village. First, they stopped off at Mr Crock's cottage and told him all about Sheltie's find.

Mr Crock was in his garden tending to his vegetables when Sheltie's head appeared over the stone wall and surprised him with a loud raspberry.

'Well done, Sheltie,' said Mr Crock when he heard how Emma's little pony had been the one to find Chalky. 'What we need to do now is organize a party of helpers to restore the chalk pony to his full glory, grazing up on Barrow Hill. The council will have to think again once they see Chalky.'

'I'll go and tell Mum straight away,' said Emma. 'She's brilliant at organizing things.'

When Mum and Dad heard about how

Sheltie had found the chalk pony, they were delighted. And just as excited as Emma and Sally.

'This is exactly what we need,' said Mum. 'I shall write a letter to the council straight away and tell them to think again. The new road will have to go *around* the hill now!'

'And I'll telephone some of our friends in the village and organize some helpers,' said Dad.

'We can ask all our friends too,' said Emma. 'I'm sure they'll want to help. There's Alice Parker, Dylan, Robert and Tracy. They've all got ponies, so it'll be easy for them to get up to the hill.'

'That's a point,' said Dad. 'It might not be so easy for some people to get to the hill. It's a long way on foot.'

'But it's easy on ponies,' said Emma excitedly. 'Come on, Sally, we'll round up our own helpers. Sheltie and Minnow have friends too!'

'You'd both better have some lunch first,' said Mum. 'I'll telephone home for you, Sally, and tell your parents that you're eating with us. Would you like that?'

'Yes please,' beamed Sally.

The two girls exchanged grins and began making plans as to who they should call on first.

Chapter Five

Later that afternoon, Emma and Sally were back up on the hill with their friends Robert, Dylan, Alice and Tracy.

Everyone wanted to help and they all sat on their ponies, talking about the task ahead.

Sheltie was already pawing away at the grass again with his hoofs. He seemed to really enjoy this new game, and couldn't wait to get started.

'It's a shame Mr Crock is too old to climb the hill,' said Emma. 'But it was nice of him to lend us the garden rakes and hoes to help scrape away the grass.'

Emma's friends slipped off their ponies and set to work.

It was much harder than they had first thought. Some of the brambles were really thick and the weeds were deeply rooted.

But they carried on and worked for a good hour before Emma's dad arrived with some other helpers. Sheltie discovered that if he trampled the weeds hard with his feet first, then they came away much easier when he pawed with his front hoofs.

'Hello, everyone,' called Dad when he arrived. 'You all know Mr Samson from the sweet shop. And Todd Wallace. And this is Mike, Todd's friend from the

garage.' Nobody
else Dad had telephoned could
get away. They had all said they had
things to do and promised to try and come
by the following day – Sunday.

Dad had also brought with him a picnic
tea and a treat for the ponies. Emma
thought it was wonderful, sitting up on the
hill having a picnic. From the top of the hill
they could look down across the whole of
Little Applewood, just like the chalk pony.

When they had finished eating, everyone
stood around looking at Chalky. They had

all worked really hard and managed to uncover more than half the chalk pony.

'A pony cut out of the chalk hill,' smiled Todd. 'You don't see many of them around the country these days. Nobody makes them any more. This chalk pony must be very special.'

'And it belongs to Little Applewood,' said Mr Samson.

'And so does the hill,' added Emma. Sheltie pushed his chin on to Emma's shoulder. He could tell that Emma was excited about something, and wanted to be included. 'The council won't be allowed to flatten the hill now, will they?' she said.

'Let's hope not,' said Dad. 'We'll just have to wait and see. But I expect they won't once they read Mum's letter and see the petition. They're certain to want to come and look for themselves.'

'When will they come?' asked Emma. 'I hope we have time to finish it first!'

'I'm sure we will,' said Todd. 'The council don't do anything very quickly.'

It was Dad's idea to pile all the weeds and grass into a heap and have a bonfire. Emma and Sheltie stood back while Dad carefully lit the fire.

A thin wisp of smoke rose into the sky as the pile of weeds and brambles slowly burned. Sheltie watched as tiny sparks crackled and popped. The pile burned and grew smaller and smaller until nothing was left but ashes.

Before they left, Dad made certain that the fire was out and spread the ashes with a rake across the shoulders and head of the chalk pony.

Sheltie helped and stomped on the cool embers with his hoofs.

'It's all grey now,' said Emma. 'It's supposed to be white!'

'She's a clever one, that Emma of yours,' laughed Todd. 'And she's right. When Chalky is all cleared away we shall have to carry clean, fresh chalk from the pit and spread it over him. That'll show the council.'

Emma was thrilled with the idea.

Sheltie threw back his head and called with a series of loud whinnies.

'We can use Sheltie's fish cart to carry the chalk,' suggested Emma. 'Sheltie would love to help out!'

'But first we've got to clear the rest,' said Todd. 'Then I'll cut a new outline before we spread the clean chalk.'

'We'll come back tomorrow,' said Dad.
'And try and bring as many helpers as we
can!' Then everyone packed up and went
back down to the village and home.

Emma and Sheltie stayed up on the hill
with Dad for a while, and watched the sun
set behind the trees on a distant rise.

It was beautiful. Little Applewood had
never seemed so special.

Chapter Six

Emma could hardly wait for the next day
to come. All that hard work up on the hill
had tired her out. But she was so excited,
even though she barely had enough
strength to turn Sheltie out into his
paddock.

Emma rubbed Sheltie down until her
arms ached, then gave him a kiss as she
said goodnight.

'You were brilliant today, boy. If

everyone works as hard as you, we'll soon have the job finished.'

When Emma went to bed she fell asleep as soon as her head hit the pillow.

Emma woke on Sunday morning to the sound of rain pelting against her bedroom window.

'Oh no!' she said aloud as she sat up in bed. She rushed to the window and looked outside. The sky was thick with dark, ragged clouds and the rain was pouring down. She could see Sheltie in the paddock peering out of his field shelter. He didn't want to come outside at all. It looked as though it had been raining for hours.

When Emma went downstairs, Mum was in the kitchen preparing a picnic lunch to take up to the hill.

'I thought I'd pack a basket, just in case,' said Mum. 'But this rain looks as if it's settled.'

'I hope not,' moaned Emma. 'We're supposed to be up on the hill all day, working on Chalky.'

'I know,' said Mum. 'But we won't be going anywhere in this weather.'

'Still, you never know,' said Dad, trying to sound cheerful. 'The rain could stop at any minute.'

Mum looked at Dad and raised a doubtful eyebrow as she finished packing the basket, just in case!

After breakfast Emma went outside to see Sheltie. It was still raining hard and Emma pulled up the hood of her waterproof as she squelched down the garden to the paddock. Rain or not, Sheltie still needed feeding.

When Sheltie saw Emma coming he blew a loud snort as if to say, 'About time, I'm starving!' And when Emma reached the shelter, the little pony shook out his wet mane and showered her in the face with raindrops.

'Eurgh!' squealed Emma. Sheltie's eyes twinkled with mischief. 'I bet you did that on purpose.' Emma pushed past him into the shelter. It was nice and dry in there.

Emma scooped pony mix into his feed manger and watched Sheltie gobble down the lot in seconds. Then she pulled some hay from his net and hand-fed him while she listened to the rain pounding on the tin roof.

'What a pity it's raining, Sheltie. You were so clever to find the chalk pony yesterday and now it looks as if we won't be able to go back up there at all today.'

Sheltie looked out at the rain too and harrumphed as if he agreed. Then he nuzzled up to Emma as they both waited for the rain to stop.

But the rain didn't stop. It continued to pour all morning.

'Seeing as I've prepared a picnic basket,' said Mum, 'we may as well have it here in the kitchen.'

Dad laid the table and they all sat down to sandwiches, sausage rolls and cake. Emma saved a little bit of her cake as a treat for Sheltie.

After lunch she put up an umbrella and walked down to the paddock with Joshua.

'Sheltie has stayed inside his shelter all morning,' said Emma. 'This weather's too wet and miserable even for you, isn't it, boy?'

Sheltie grunted and blew through his lips miserably.

Emma and Joshua fed Sheltie his cake treat, then went back indoors.

Later that afternoon the rain did finally stop.

'But it will be too wet to do any work on the chalk pony,' said Dad.

Nevertheless, Emma decided to take Sheltie out for some exercise, and sploshed him through all the puddles as they rode over to Sally's house.

The two girls walked their ponies down the muddy lanes and talked about all the work that still needed doing up on the hill. Sheltie nuzzled up to Minnow and nibbled at his mane as they ambled along.

'We can talk to the others at school tomorrow and organize a special work party after class,' said Emma.

'That's a good idea,' agreed Sally. 'It doesn't start getting dark until eight. We can do quite a lot of work before then if all our friends turn up.'

But the following day, everyone didn't turn up. Alice and Tracy couldn't come. And neither could some of the others.

That left only Emma, Sally, Dylan and Robert.

Sheltie flicked his mane and looked around him. He liked being up on the hill with all his pony friends.

Sheltie helped Emma with the weed clearing again. His hoofs were perfect for scraping.

But the other three ponies weren't interested and just stood chomping grass.

Nearly all the chalk pony was uncovered now, apart from his back legs and tail. But his new outline still needed cutting, and with all the rain he was a dirty grey colour. The chalk in the pit was all damp too, so they would have to wait for that to dry out in the sunshine before they could start collecting it.

*

On Tuesday morning, Mum received a letter from the council. She read it aloud at the breakfast table.

'Dear Mrs Matthews,' she began. 'Thank you for your letter about the chalk pony on Barrow Hill. Unfortunately, our offices can find no record of such a landmark, but would be interested in visiting the site as soon as possible before roadworks begin.

'However, if the latest plans for re-routing the new road are to be abandoned, the council will naturally expect the chalk pony to be in good condition and able to pass our surveyor's inspection.

'In the duty of public interest we shall be sending our chief officer to inspect the site and write a full report this coming Friday morning.'

'Friday morning!' gasped Emma. 'But

that's only three days away. We'll never finish the chalk pony in three days. And we can only work for a few hours in the evenings after school.' Her face dropped.

'You're right,' said Dad. 'It's not much time at all, is it? And, as the letter says, if the chalk pony isn't in good condition when the inspector comes, they'll just go ahead, flatten the hill and build the road!'

'They can't,' said Mum. 'Surely they will be able to see that the chalk pony is an important part of the landscape. Even if it is only half finished!'

'But the council doesn't like being told that they can't do things,' said Dad. 'It will be their way of getting out of it if Chalky isn't finished in time.'

'Then we'll just have to make sure that he is,' said Mum.

But how? thought Emma.

She worried about it all the way as she walked to school.

And that morning, when the first lesson began in class, Emma was still thinking hard.

Chapter Seven

Miss Jenkins handed out paper and set the class to work.

'I want you all to write an essay about village life,' she said.

Emma knew straight away what she was going to write. Her essay would be all about the new road and how Sheltie had found the chalk pony up on Barrow Hill.

When the class had finished, Miss Jenkins collected all the papers and flipped through them, looking for one to read out loud for the second lesson.

Emma held her breath and waited to see which one the teacher would choose. She hoped it would be hers.

Emma didn't have to wait long. Miss Jenkins picked out an essay and settled the class as she prepared to read.

'"The Pony on the Hill", by Emma Matthews,' she began.

Emma shot a glance across to Sally and beamed her friend a wide grin.

'That was an excellent story,' said Miss Jenkins when she had finished reading. All the class thought so too and clapped noisily. Emma felt her face burning red.

'I think everyone enjoyed that,' smiled the teacher. 'And I think Sheltie's

discovery of the chalk pony was fantastic. But I thought it was very sad at the end, when Emma told us how, after all the hard work, there might not be enough time to finish the pony before the council inspector's visit on Friday.'

'It's not fair,' piped up Josie Phillips. 'Can't we do something about it?'

This gave Miss Jenkins an idea.

'As it's such a lovely day outside,' she said, 'why don't we all go up to Barrow Hill this afternoon and take our nature lesson in the sunshine?'

The whole class yelled at once. 'Yes!'

'Do you still have all the tools at home that Mr Crock lent you, Emma?' asked the teacher.

'Oh, yes, miss,' said Emma brightly.

'Then why don't you go home at lunchtime, with Sally, and bring them up to the hill this afternoon. I'm sure there are enough willing hands here to finish the job you started. What does the class think?'

A sudden outburst of cheers was the answer.

'And can I bring Sheltie?' asked Emma. 'He can help me fetch the tools. I can put everything in his little cart. He won't be in the way, I promise! And he's brilliant at scraping weeds.'

'That's a wonderful idea, Emma,' said Miss Jenkins. 'I'm sure Sheltie will be an enormous help. After all, it was Sheltie who found the chalk pony in the first place, wasn't it?'

At lunchtime, Emma and Sally ran all the way home to the cottage. Mum was surprised to see them. Normally Emma ate her packed lunch at school.

Sheltie was excited to see Emma. He raced around the paddock in a mad dash and couldn't stand still for a second. When Mum heard what Miss Jenkins was planning she was thrilled.

Emma and Sally ate the contents of their

lunch boxes sitting on the paddock fence while Mum got Sheltie ready.

Sheltie would sooner have snaffled one of Emma's sandwiches. But he stood still for Mum instead, while she harnessed him to his little cart and loaded up all the tools. She put in some extra ones too. A spade, a rake and two garden hoes.

Mum was just as excited as Emma, and said that she would drive over to Marjorie's later and see if Todd Wallace could come and help too.

Emma, Sally and Sheltie set off with the cartload of tools and headed towards Barrow Hill.

When they got there, Miss Jenkins and the whole class were standing in a circle looking down at the chalk pony.

'None of us has ever seen it before,' said

51

the teacher. 'And although it isn't finished, we all think it's wonderful, just like in your story, Emma!'

Sheltie blew an extra loud snort when he saw all Emma's classmates. Everyone rushed over to pet and fuss him. Sheltie loved all the attention, and nuzzled into as many sweatshirts as he could find, looking for peppermints.

'Come on, Sheltie,' said Emma, finally. 'We've got work to do.'

Miss Jenkins looked at all the tools, and helped Emma and Sally to unload them from Sheltie's cart.

'I'll slip Sheltie from his harness,' said Emma, 'and let him stand free so that he can help.'

'Right, you lot,' said Miss Jenkins. She organized three groups, and soon had the first group scraping away at the weeds and brambles with rakes and hoes.

Sheltie helped, and used his feet again to scrape away at the grass. His little hoofs could move faster than any garden tools.

'Second group,' announced Miss Jenkins, 'pick up all the brambles and weeds and pile them in a big heap over there. And, group three, use your trowels and forks to dig up any clumps of grass that are left behind.'

Sheltie was having such a good time pawing at any stray patches of grass he could find. And it wasn't long, with all the extra help, before the chalk pony's hind legs and tail were cleared and his whole shape was visible. Every weed, bramble and clump of grass had been raked away to reveal Chalky in his full glory.

'All we need now,' said Emma, 'is for Mr Wallace to cut a clean outline. Then we can start spreading the fresh chalk.'

And as if Todd Wallace had heard what Emma had just said, he suddenly appeared, striding over the crest of the hill, with Emma's mum and Joshua in tow.

Sheltie blew a lively snort and raced over to greet them both.

Joshua squealed when he saw Sheltie. The little pony gently nuzzled Joshua's hand with his soft muzzle.

Then Sheltie pulled at the bag Mum was carrying and became so excited by the smell of carrots that he gave himself hiccups.

Chapter Eight

'Hello, everyone,' called Mum. 'I've brought along Mr Wallace to help.'

Sheltie went over to sniff at Todd Wallace and see if there were any mints hidden in his pockets.

'Well, it looks like you've all been working very hard,' observed Mum.

'They've all been absolutely brilliant,' said Miss Jenkins. 'And Sheltie's been helping too! His hoofs are like mechanical shovels.'

Sheltie pricked up his ears when he heard his name and blew a loud raspberry which came out as a 'hic!' and made the teacher laugh.

'You're cheekier than any of my pupils, Sheltie,' she said. Sheltie pushed his head against her arm and blew softly through his lips.

Todd took over the organization from Miss Jenkins. 'The first thing to do,' he said, 'is to light a fire in Chalky's belly and burn that pile of weeds. Then we can spread the ashes and set down a new bed for the fresh chalk.'

The small bonfire burned quickly, and while Mum and Miss Jenkins kept an eye on everyone, Todd began work, cutting a

clean, sharp outline for Barrow Hill's new chalk pony with a special spade.

'When I've finished,' he smiled, 'I'll put out the fire and rake the ashes. I should be done in an hour or two.'

Miss Jenkins decided to lead the class back down to the school. They had done all they could for one day.

It was up to Todd now. Emma and Sheltie went straight home with Mum and Joshua. All the tools had been loaded back into Sheltie's little cart. Joshua toddled alongside, clapping his hands and yelling excitedly. 'Gee up, Sheltie. Gee up.'

When they arrived back home, Emma led Sheltie into his paddock and glanced up at Barrow Hill.

The late afternoon sunshine was drying out all the ashes to a pale grey. And now that Todd had spread them, Chalky looked almost white. The pony's shape was neatly outlined against the green grass of the hill and Emma saw Little Applewood's chalk pony really clearly for the first time.

'Doesn't he look fantastic?' said Emma. 'Up there, grazing on the hilltop.'

'And to think,' said Mum, 'that he was up there all the time and none of us knew!'

'Mr Crock knew,' Emma reminded Mum.

'Yes, he did, didn't he?' Mum smiled. 'But it was you and Sheltie who found him. What a clever pair you are.'

Sheltie looked towards the hill too. He cocked his head to the side and harrumphed gently to himself.

That evening, Miss Jenkins had another surprise for everyone. She telephoned Mum and asked if Emma could bring Sheltie and his little cart along to school ving day.

to Mr Price, the

60

headmaster,' said Miss Jenkins, 'and he's given the class the whole day off. We're all going back up to the hill tomorrow to finish the job. Do you think you could contact Mr Wallace and get him to come along too?'

'I'm sure I can,' said Mum. 'He's as eager to finish Chalky as we all are.'

'Oh, and another thing,' said the teacher. 'No school uniform tomorrow. Just old clothes – jeans and a T-shirt or something.'

She hung up the phone and Mum called Todd Wallace straight away.

Emma could hardly believe her ears when she heard the news!

Chapter Nine

The next day, after breakfast, Emma loaded Sheltie's little cart with all the tools. Then she bundled up a pile of old plastic bags, placed them on top, and was ready.

Sheltie knew he was going somewhere and was already acting frisky. He bobbed his head and nudged Emma gently.

Emma felt really excited about taking Sheltie to school again.

'I wish you could be in our class every day,' said Emma. But she knew that today was special and decided to enjoy every moment of the journey.

As they passed Mr Crock's cottage Sheltie blew an excited snort and made the old man pop his head up over the garden wall.

'Hello,' called Mr Crock. 'And where are two going?'

'We're off to school,' grinned Emma.

'My, my,' smiled Mr Crock. 'I've never heard of a pony taking lessons before.'

Emma laughed, then told Mr Crock all about their mission.

Mr Crock was delighted. 'Looks as though the hill will be saved after all,' he chuckled. 'Good luck, Emma. And well done, Sheltie.' He passed a nice juicy

carrot over the wall for the little pony and laughed as Sheltie crunched away noisily on his treat.

Sheltie was full of beans this morning. His trot was extra frisky as he pulled the little cart all the way to the school.

Miss Jenkins had gathered everyone in the small playground to wait for Emma and Sheltie. The class gathered round

Sheltie and made a big fuss of him again.

Miss Jenkins had some apples in a bag for the children to feed to Sheltie later on. Sheltie spotted the bag straight away and stood in front of the teacher with his ears pricked and his head cocked at a cheeky angle.

'They're not for eating now,' smiled Miss Jenkins as she hid the bag behind her back. Sheltie gave a low whicker and looked a bit disappointed.

'Don't be greedy, Sheltie,' said Emma. She gave his chin a good scratch to distract him. 'You can have an apple when you've done some work.'

Todd Wallace was already up on the hill, waiting for his helpers.

'I've worked out that it will take at least

twenty bags full of chalk to freshen up this chalk pony,' he said when the class turned up.

'Twenty bags have to be filled and loaded into Sheltie's little cart,' he added. 'Then Sheltie can pull the cart and bring the chalk over for me to spread around.'

The chalk pit itself was only a short distance away. It was a shallow basin scooped out of the hill, and sloped down steeply on one side.

'The easiest way to collect the chalk,' announced Miss Jenkins, 'is to climb down the gentler slope and approach the pit from the bottom. I've got six small shovels for you to use, so take turns and no squabbling!'

Sally led the class down into the pit. Emma stayed up on the top with Sheltie.

When the bags were ready, the little pony was going to help Emma and pull them up, one by one, on a rope.

Sheltie kept a watchful eye on everyone as they took turns shovelling white dusty chalk into the bags.

'That looks like great fun,' said Emma.

There was lots of shrieking and heaps of mess as Emma's class worked.

'Look at all that powdery chalk flying everywhere, Sheltie!' she said. 'It's a good job we're all wearing old clothes today.'

Sheltie rolled back his lips and gave his version of a pony laugh.

Within minutes the enthusiastic workers below were covered from head to foot in white powder.

'Now they look like ghosts with their white hands and faces,' laughed Emma.

Suddenly Sheltie became quite frisky. He could see Sally and the others down in the pit having such a great time shovelling and filling bags. The little Shetland pony wanted to be down there too!

Before Emma could stop him, Sheltie pulled his cart to the edge of the pit and peered down into the basin.

'No, Sheltie!' called Emma. 'Come back!'

She hurried over to grab his reins, but Sheltie already had his front legs on the steep, chalky slope.

As Emma pulled on the reins she felt Sheltie slide a little away from her.

'No!' said Emma again, very sternly. 'Stop, Sheltie!'

Below in the pit, Josie Phillips suddenly looked up and screamed. It looked as if Sheltie was about to slide down the slope on top of her, cart and all!

But luckily Sheltie stopped still. One more step and he would have slipped down into the chalk pit.

'Phew! That was close,' breathed Emma. 'For a minute I thought Sheltie was going to slide all the way to the bottom.'

'He nearly did,' said Todd, who was

near by. 'You'd better keep a closer eye on him, Emma.'

Emma looked at her shoes and felt her face turn red.

The incident was soon forgotten and the first load of five bags was hauled up on ropes and piled into Sheltie's cart. The little pony did his job of pulling the cart up and across the crest of the hill. Todd Wallace took the bags one by one and tipped them out into the belly of the chalk pony.

Sheltie saw the mound of white powder close up for the first time, and stared at it quizzically. He pushed his nose into the white mound and gave a tremendous sneeze. The chalk powder blew everywhere. Sheltie looked as though someone had tipped a bag of flour over his head. Now the little pony looked like a ghost too!

Sheltie had such a surprised expression on his face that Emma burst out laughing. Then Sheltie snorted and nudged her playfully with his chalky muzzle.

Emma toppled backwards and sat down on the chalk mound with a soft thud.

Todd adjusted his cap and grinned. 'We're supposed to be spreading it, not squashing it, Emma!' he said with a wink.

Emma struggled to her feet and wiped her hands on her jeans. She was covered now too! 'Look what you've gone and done,' she laughed. 'What a mess, Sheltie!'

Sheltie blinked and fluttered his long chalk-covered lashes.

'Never mind,' said Todd. 'Go and fetch some more while I start spreading this lot.'

Sheltie left white hoof marks all across
the green grass as he pulled the cart back
to the chalk pit.

Five more bags were filled and waiting.
It didn't take long before all the chalk was
tipped out and spread across the pony-
shape cut out of the hill.

When they had finished, everyone stood back to admire their work.

'Now Chalky looks clean, fresh and white, just as he's meant to look,' said Emma. But it was difficult to see what he looked like properly because they were all standing too near. Chalky wasn't a very big pony, but he was best viewed from some distance away.

Miss Jenkins gathered the class together. 'Come on, we'll walk in a line away from the chalk pony to a higher rise where you can all see him better.'

The chalk pony looked splendid from a short distance away.

The children had walked back, and were just about to settle down with their picnic lunches when Sheltie started blowing a very loud ripple of noisy snorts. His ears

pricked up and he stared down the hill at
the figure of a man in a dark suit climbing
his way up the hill.

'Miss Jenkins,' called Emma. 'Someone's
coming!'

Chapter Ten

The teacher squinted into the bright
sunshine and saw the man coming up
towards them.

'I wonder who that is?' said Emma.

'It's not one of the teachers,' answered
Sally. 'I've never seen him before. I
wonder what he wants.'

The man was short, dumpy and very
round. He carried a briefcase and
struggled, huffing and puffing, up on to

the rise. His face was very red and shiny.

'Good afternoon,' he said, breathing heavily. He spoke in a strict, gruff voice. 'I'm Mr Carp, from the council.'

'The council!' exclaimed Miss Jenkins. 'But you're not expected until Friday.'

'Change of schedule,' said Mr Carp coldly. 'This afternoon's meeting was cancelled, so I thought I'd use the opportunity of inspecting the site earlier than planned.' He flipped open his briefcase and took out a clipboard. Then he looked at the chalk pony and muttered something under his breath. 'Hmm! Just as I thought.'

Next, he glanced round and studied Emma's classmates. They were still all covered in white chalk and looking like a bunch of spooks.

He returned his attention to the clipboard, scribbled some notes, then cleared his throat.

'Are you in charge here?' he addressed Miss Jenkins. The teacher smiled politely and nodded.

'As you may know,' he began, 'the council planning office has no record of a chalk pony landmark on Barrow Hill or any other hill in the area.' As he spoke, he made some more notes on his clipboard.

'And after this surprise inspection of this site,' he said, 'I believe that the reason there are no records is because there never was a chalk pony here in the first place.'

'But it's there!' said Emma, puzzled. 'You can see it for yourself in front of you.'

Sheltie put his head down too and

poked his muzzle into the fresh chalk which Todd had just finished spreading. Then he sneezed and blew a cloud of white powder all over Mr Carp's dark trousers.

Mr Carp was very annoyed.

'Just look at this mess,' he snapped, brushing the chalk from his trousers. 'It's quite obvious to me from looking at you all, that you have only just finished this so-called landmark. And that you've tried to pretend to the council that it was here all along in order to stop the new road going ahead.

'It's a good job I came two days early,' Mr Carp continued. 'I've caught you lot red-handed.' His gaze fell upon the pile of shovels covered in white chalk. He made yet another note on his clipboard.

Miss Jenkins opened her mouth to speak, but quickly closed it again and said nothing.

Emma suddenly realized what the situation must have looked like. One freshly cut, freshly chalked pony, looking sparkling white and brand new. Sixteen children covered in white powder. A pony and cart filled with empty, chalky bags. A pile of shovels. And Todd, standing in the middle of the landmark with a rake in his hand.

It was Todd who spoke out. 'We didn't make it,' he said curtly. 'We just sweetened it. Freshened it up a little. It's been here for years and years.'

Mr Carp smirked. 'You're going to have quite a job proving that!' he said. 'And by the time I've finished my report, I don't think the council will believe anything you've got to say about the matter.'

Sheltie's ears went flat. He didn't like this man's voice. It was very loud. He didn't like the man either, so he leaned forward and blew a really loud snort.

Mr Carp backed away. He seemed to be frightened of Sheltie. And what happened next happened so quickly that no one could stop it. Not even Emma.

Sheltie gave a loud sneeze, and Mr Carp hopped backwards in fright. With one final snort from Sheltie, the council inspector lost his balance and tumbled backwards into the chalk pit.

Over and over he rolled, down the sloping side of the shallow chalk basin, where he landed with a soft thud at the bottom.

Everyone rushed to the top of the pit
and looked down at the council inspector.

Some of the children couldn't help
giggling. Mr Carp did look funny, lying on
his back, covered in chalk and kicking his
legs in the air.

'Oh, Sheltie,' said Emma. 'Look what
you've done now!'

Sheltie looked down at Mr Carp and
blew a final loud raspberry.

Chapter Eleven

It was Todd who came to the rescue. He lowered a rope into the pit and organized everyone into a tug of war at one end. Even Sheltie helped. He grabbed the rope with his teeth and pulled as Mr Carp struggled at the other end of the rope.

Very slowly, they pulled the council inspector up and out of the pit.

When Mr Carp at last stood safely on top of the hill, he snapped at Miss Jenkins.

'I've hurt my ankle. You'll have to help me get back to my car.'

Suddenly, Emma interrupted. 'Sheltie can help,' she offered. 'You can ride back down the hill in Sheltie's cart.'

Mr Carp looked horrified.

'I don't think so!' he said rudely. 'I'm not going anywhere near that animal!'

'Then you'll just have to stay up here,' said Todd. 'There's no other way down!'

There was no other choice. Mr Carp had to ride back down to the village in Sheltie's little cart.

Miss Jenkins and the children followed behind in silence, carrying the tools as Emma led the way. Mr Carp moaned about his ankle the whole time.

At the foot of the hill, Emma glanced round to look back up at the chalk pony.

It didn't seem fair that after all their
hard work it looked as if the hill would be
flattened anyway. Then she had an idea!

She steered Sheltie to the right and
began running with him up the lane.

'Hey! Where are you going?' yelled Mr
Carp. 'My car's over there!' But Emma
took no notice.

'Stop!' called Mr Carp. 'Stop this pony at once!' But again, Emma took no notice and trotted Sheltie along, with the cart bumping behind him. Even when Miss Jenkins called out, Emma ran on. The entire class had to follow Emma and Sheltie up the lane.

It didn't take long before Sheltie reached Mr Crock's cottage. Then Emma finally stopped and pulled up Sheltie to a halt.

'What on earth are you doing?' grumbled Mr Carp. Emma left Sheltie and raced into Mr Crock's garden.

'Mr Crock! Mr Crock!' called Emma. 'Come quickly.'

Mr Crock rushed out from his potting shed to see what all the fuss was about. He looked over the wall and saw Mr Carp sitting in Sheltie's cart.

'Well, well, well,' said Mr Crock. 'If it isn't young Carpy.'

'Young Carpy?' said Emma. She seemed puzzled, but quickly told Mr Crock what had happened and urged him to show the old photograph of the chalk pony to the council inspector.

Mr Crock hurried inside, then quickly came out again with the photo album.

Sheltie stomped his feet excitedly and gave a loud blow. He knew something important was going on.

'This will prove that Chalky has been up on the hill for years and years,' Emma said triumphantly. And it did.

Mr Crock opened the album for Mr Carp to see and jabbed at the photograph with his finger.

'There!' he said. 'There's the chalk pony.'

Then he pointed out the three figures in the foreground.

'That's me. That's Fred Berry. And that, young Carpy,' he said flatly, pointing to the third man, 'is your father.'

Chapter Twelve

There was no mistaking it. Mr Carp
looked at the photograph and recognized
his father straight away. And he could see
the chalk pony quite clearly up on the hill
in the distance, behind them.

'What have you got to say about that
then?' asked Mr Crock.

There was nothing that could be said.
The inspector had to agree that the chalk
pony must have been there for years and

years after all. The photograph proved it beyond doubt.

'I'm sorry for bumping you down the lane,' said Emma. 'But it was the only way. I wanted you to see the photo for yourself.'

Mr Carp seemed to have a change of heart once he had seen the old photograph. At first his face turned red. Then he coughed and faced Emma and the rest of the class who by this time had gathered around him.

'Well, it seems as if I may have jumped to the wrong conclusion,' he said. 'But I was only doing my job.'

'Does that mean that you believe us after all?' said Emma.

'I suppose so,' answered Mr Carp. 'The photograph does cast an entirely different light on the matter.' Then he opened his briefcase, took out his clipboard and tore off the sheet of paper with his scribbled notes.

Sheltie pushed in quickly and snaffled the notes from Mr Carp's hand. Then he chewed at the paper and began to eat it.

Mr Carp smiled. 'It's all right, Sheltie. We won't be needing that any more. I shall write a whole new report and the chalk pony will stay exactly where he is. The new road will have to go around the hill after all.'

Sheltie snorted so excitedly that he made himself belch. Everyone laughed. Sheltie could be so funny.

'I don't know why I was so frightened of him,' smiled the inspector as he stroked Sheltie's soft velvet muzzle.

'Sheltie's as gentle as a lamb,' said Emma.

Sheltie whinnied loudly and everyone looked up, across to Barrow Hill. The chalk pony stood white and proud, looking down over the village of Little Applewood.

He looked as though he had been there for ever, as in fact he had.

'You know who that chalk pony reminds me of?' said Mr Carp.

'SHELTIE!' cried Emma and her friends together. And they were right.

'Looks like it's Sheltie for ever!' said Miss Jenkins.

Emma had never felt so proud.